S0-BUC-095

Other books by Gerard Rose

The Early Troubles

The Boy Captain

Bless Me Father

For I Have Sinned

A Western Hero

Hamilton & Egberta

The War to End

The War to End

By Gerard Rose

Carmel, California

April 2018

This book is a work of fiction based on historical fact. You are invited to both enjoy and learn from the story.

The War to End

All Rights Reserved

Copyright © 2018 by Gerard Rose

No part of this book may be reproduced or transmitted in any form or by any means, electronic or mechanical, including photocopying, recording, or by any information storage and retrieval system, without permission in writing from the Seton Publishing. For more information about the author, go to GerardRose.com.

Published by SetonPublishing.com.

ISBN-13: 978-0-9989605-5-5
ISBN-10: 0-9989605-5-1

Printed in the United States of America

Table of Contents

Publisher's Note

It is such a pleasure to receive a new manuscript from Gerard Rose. This is the seventh that he has submitted to me for publication, and it is truly an honor to present such fine writing and important thought.

This book is written in a unique style, different from Gerard's previous work. My experience reading it the first time was that I could hear him thinking the words out loud, giving particular significance to those words that were important in the time this story takes place.

Another winning point is that he starts off with a story of a grave and historic era. He makes two young men players in that time. And then he makes their lives the story. Amazing lives that in many ways define the life of this nation.

This latest work of historical fiction is based on real people in Gerard's life, friends and family. Most of what isn't pure fact is based on fact, and is employed to more richly define the circumstances of this ugly period in our history.

That ugliness has increasingly resurfaced over the past couple of years, "legitimized" and encouraged by the campaign and presidency of a man who has openly expressed racist attitudes against people based simply on their ancestry, skin color, or religion.

Gerard's *The War to End* will remind some readers and inform others of the discrimination that was brutally practiced against people from Japan, and Germany, countries that are today principal allies.

It is important that we know our history – especially those chapters we would prefer to hide in ignorance or denial – so that we don't find ourselves repeating behavior of the worst parts of our nature.

If we are ever to restore luster to our self image of the shining city on the hill, we must not only know the truth of our actions like the internment of the Americans of Japanese ancestry, but we must look deep into our personal and national souls for the flaws that made these actions possible.

Only this will we heal our wounds and prevent such crimes from ever being committed again.

Thank you, Gerard, for *The War to End.*

Tony Seton
Carmel, California

Author's Note

Although this work is based on actual events and real people, it has been properly designated as "fiction." I say that because some events depicted here have been combined, abbreviated, or fictionalized, and because several names have been changed to protect privacy rights and/or recast stories based on differing recollections of what actually happened.

Even today, many of the few remaining veterans of World War II are reluctant to talk about their experiences. So too, many Nisei and their descendants are reluctant to discuss the relocation of Japanese Americans during the War, mostly because they consider themselves loyal Americans, and do not wish to portray the Country they love in a negative light. But the basic facts relating to War itself, and to Presidential Order 9066 and its aftermath, are absolutely true, and deserve to be told so that – if for no other reason – history won't repeat itself.

Gerard Rose
Carmel, California

<u>*Dedication*</u>

To my daughter Camille, in the hope that her generation will take appropriate steps to assure that we never experience another war like World War II, nor a breakdown of civil liberties as occurred at the outset of that terrible conflict.

Preface

As a veteran of the Vietnam War, and as a former Naval Officer, I saw firsthand some of the racial prejudices that were infecting our country during that period. This novel addresses similar prejudices at an earlier place and time, but the lesson then, as now, remains the same: treating our fellow Americans unequally because of their race is basically inconsistent with our core values.

The War to End

1 - *The Beginning*

It was still dark on a cool Monday morning in December of 1941, and Robert Rose and his best friend, Raymond Ishimatsu, were about to board a train that would take them from Berkeley to San Jose. There they planned to spend the week together with Raymond's family, which farmed approximately one hundred acres of peach and apple trees in rural Cupertino, a small village in the hills above San Jose that separate the San Francisco Bay from the central coast of California.

Robert's maternal grandparents lived a short distance away from San Jose in Santa Cruz, a small beach town on the central coast that was famous for its Boardwalk and for a giant roller coaster called the Big Dipper that had been built on the Boardwalk in 1924.

Robert's paternal grandmother, Dora Rose, was a Gold Star mother who lived with her daughter, Madeline, and Madeline's husband, Claude Bradley, in Corralitos, which is located in the Santa Cruz Mountains south of Santa Cruz. Claude was a World War I veteran who spent most of the War in France, and was a close friend of Madeline's brother Donald, who was killed in Saint

Mihel, France, during the Chateau Thiery offensive in August of 1918[1].

Robert, who was born on his grandparent's ranch in Santa Cruz in 1916, and Raymond, who was slightly younger than Robert[2], were roommates in one of several "co-op" dormitories at the University of California[3]. The idea of the co-ops was that the residents, all of whom were graduate students, would spend at least ten hours per week washing dishes, and assisting one another in the cleaning and upkeep of the buildings. For their efforts, residents would thereby earn a discount from the University on their tuition, room, and board.

Robert and Raymond had collaborated on their final theses for doctorate degrees in entomology[4], and they were waiting for input from their faculty advisers about final changes to their submissions – which included epidemiological research the two of them had collaborated on which dealt with the spread and detection of

---

1. See "A Western Hero" (Seton Publishing, April, 2015).

2. Robert had taken a brief time off from school after he received his Bachelor of Science degree at UC in order to earn money to pay for the cost of his graduate studies at Berkeley.

3. According to Robert, his total cost for room and board at the co-ops was set at $12 per month.

4. Entomology is the scientific study of insects.

tropical diseases generally, and malaria in particular[5].

A fierce war had already engulfed most of Europe, and rumors of possible involvement by the United States left many young men, including Robert and Raymond, uncertain about their futures.

As they waited at the Berkeley train station, Robert wanted to read the latest sports news, and he looked around for one of the newsboys who normally parked themselves alongside departing trains. But for some reason, on this morning, none of the newsboys was anywhere to be seen.

The University and many other businesses in downtown Berkeley were closed for Christmas break, and except for a few tourists, the station was virtually empty.

Were he not visiting Raymond's family, Robert would probably have taken the train all the way over to the Coast, and spent some time with his grandparents in Santa Cruz.

Robert's maternal grandparents, the Prachts, had immigrated to the United States from Germany in the mid-1800s, and they spoke the German language at home. That fact, coupled with the death of Robert's uncle at the hands of German soldiers during World War I, meant that Dora Rose, Robert's paternal grandmother,

---

5. Epidemiology studies, among other things, the diagnosis and treatment of various insect borne diseases.

was ambivalent (at the very least) toward the Prachts.

For their part, the Prachts were ambivalent as well - but for different reasons. Their attitude was not grounded on anybody's ancestry, but on their fear that the United States would soon find itself at war with Germany for the second time in two and a half decades. They remembered very well that during the First World War, their neighbors made it clear that they were suspicious of, and didn't like, anyone who spoke with a German accent – much less spoke the German language.

Raymond's family, by contrast, had none of those conflicts. Everyone in his family was of Japanese descent, having moved to California, also in the mid-1800s, so they could work on the first transcontinental railroad[6].

After the railroad was completed, they had gone into farming, and had been very successful at it. They employed more than a hundred workers, and their ranch home in Cupertino was one of the largest single family dwellings in Santa Clara County.

Robert was always a welcome visitor at Raymond's home. Raymond's parents, I.K. (whom everyone called "Mr. Ishi") and Hatsuno (whom everyone called "Mom"), were impressed with Robert's knowledge of agriculture, and Raymond's sister, Carol, had a teenage

---

6. The first transcontinental railroad consisted primarily of 1,900 miles of rails, trestles and sub-grade built between Omaha, Nebraska on its eastern end and the San Francisco Bay area on its western end. The railroad was completed on May 10, 1869.

crush on Robert since she first met him on a weekend with her brother in Berkeley, several years earlier.

On their train ride to San Jose, Robert and Raymond had talked about the possibility that America might somehow become drawn into the War. According to Robert, "War with Germany is inevitable – and not altogether inappropriate. After all, the German Navy has targeted American ships, and our closest ally, Great Britain, needs our help in defending itself from Hitler."

Raymond agreed. In his mind, "There is no way this country should stand by and let our closest ally be gobbled up by a dictator."

Neither man expected a war with Japan, and certainly not that day.

But as their train pulled slowly into the downtown railway station in San Jose, they could see dozens of newsboys milling about, all waving newspapers with shocking headlines in large print: "WAR WITH THE JAPS."

Mr. Ishi, who met Robert and Raymond at the station, looked grave as he greeted them.

"Boys, I'm afraid the news is quite grim. The American naval base at Pearl Harbor has been attacked by the Japanese navy. For all practical purposes, America is now at war, not with Germany, but with Japan."

The two young men were dumfounded. "What does this mean," asked Raymond, "and how will it affect our families?"

On reflection, Robert responded that he had "a bad

feeling" about the months that lay ahead.

And as they walked toward Mr. Ishi's car, Robert couldn't help but notice that the people milling about the station were staring at both Raymond and his father, and giving them hateful looks.

2 - *Pearl Harbor*

Early on the previous morning, more than two thousand miles away in Pearl Harbor, three hundred and fifty Japanese planes under the command of Admirals Chuichi Nagumo and Isoroku Yamamoto had attacked thirty-three American ships, and inflicted more than three thousand casualties on the GI's and civilian employees of the Army and Navy who were stationed there.

In response to the attack, Mom Ishimatsu's brother, Frank Nakamoto, who was a civilian contractor working for Admiral Husband Kimmel, the Naval Commander at Pearl Harbor, had spent the longest day of his life in a small steel dingy, single-handedly pulling injured sailors from the burning waters where the ships had been tied up.

Over a period of about eight hours, he had suffered second, third and even fourth degree burns over most of his body, and his lungs were seared with pain from the heat and smoke he had ingested. His clothes were ripped and burned, and he was covered with blood and oil.

But in the course of that terrible day he had saved over seventy American boys who had jumped overboard or been blown into the water.

The devastation at Pearl Harbor was harrowing. Japanese torpedo bombs had destroyed at least three cruisers, and had caused almost unimaginable damage to most of America's Pacific fleet[7].

Alerted to the heroic rescue efforts of Frank Nakamoto, Admiral Kimmel searched for Frank and eventually found him in the intensive care unit of the Pearl Harbor Naval Hospital. Frank was barely alive, but he was awake, more or less lucid, and he was able to shake the hand of the Admiral as the latter heaped praise upon him.

"Frank," said the Admiral, "I can't tell you how relieved I am that you are alive. What you did for our boys was nothing short of miraculous. I promise, I will never forget what you did."

"Admiral," Frank responded, "I only did what any loyal American would have done."

And with that said, an exhausted Frank Nakamoto closed his eyes, and fell into a coma that would ulti-

---

7. One of the sailors pulled from the water that day was a young man from Sacramento, California named Jim Hilleary. Jim would survive the War, and one of his two children, Gilbert, would later distinguish himself as a hero while serving in Vietnam with the Army's 101st Airborne Division. After the War, Gilbert married the author's sister, Christine, and together they produced four children.

mately last for three days.

The next day, and unbeknownst to Frank, he was fired from his job at the Naval Base.

When Admiral Kimmel learned what had happened to Frank, he was appalled. In his opinion, Frank should have been awarded a medal, not terminated! He wrote to his superiors at the Pentagon and complained about Frank's treatment. But the Navy's response was a brief note that said nothing about Frank's situation, and instead questioned the Admiral's judgment in questioning the firing of a "Jap."

It turned out that Frank and all other Japanese Americans working at Pearl Harbor were fired pursuant to a General Order issued the day before by the Defense Department in Washington, D.C.

By its terms, the General Order "justified" the terminations based on "troubling facts" supposedly raised by unnamed "reliable informants" who questioned the loyalty of all Japanese Americans. From that day forward, and until the end of the War, nobody of Japanese ancestry would be allowed to work at Pearl Harbor or at any other naval facility in the United States[8].

---

8. Frank Nakamoto would later marry, and he and his wife would produce a son who was a classmate of the author at Santa Clara University's School of Law. The son, named Frank after his father, later distinguished himself as a trial lawyer specializing in the representation of underserved populations in the State of Hawaii.

As will be seen in the course of this book, the termination of Frank Nakamoto was only one among many outrages, all grounded on paranoia and racism, that would be practiced by the Government against more than a hundred thousand innocent Japanese Americans whose only "crime" was their ancestry.

3 - Government Threats

As Mr. Ishi drove Robert and Raymond from the San Jose train station toward his ranch house in Cupertino, he admitted to the young men that he was fearful for his family.

"Now that Japan is at war with the United States, there is a real danger that the American government may take punitive actions against our family. Tell me, boys, what will we do if the American Government comes after us?"[9]

Raymond nodded. "I agree father. You saw the faces of the people at the train station. They hate us, even though they don't know anything about us. It wouldn't surprise me at all if the Government tries to arrest us all. But Robert was skeptical. "I just can't believe that would happen. After all, this is America, not Nazi Germany. We have a constitution and laws that protect

---

9. A banner headline of the *San Francisco Examiner* in February 1942 read as follows: "OUSTER OF ALL JAPS IN CALIFORNIA NEAR."

us. Besides, my mom's parents were both born in Germany[10]. Could you imagine the uproar that would result if we went to war with Germany, and the Government arrested them?"[11]

Later that day, the United States formally declared war on Japan, and three days after that, Germany declared war on the United States.

As feared by Mr. Ishi, immediately after the attack on Pearl Harbor the Government began drawing up plans to evacuate all Japanese Americans living on the West Coast of the United States.

And shortly after that, the American Government came after Raymond and his family, including his mother and father.

But nobody came after Robert's family. Like most Americans at that time, Robert's immediate ancestors on both sides of his family were Caucasian and Protes-

---

10. In the mid-1800s, Robert's maternal great-grandparents, Friedrich and Mary Pracht, had immigrated to the United States from Bottingen, Germany, where the Pracht family owned a small winery, and where Friedrich had served as his town's *Burgomaster*, or mayor.

11. In fact, and unbeknownst to most Americans, the American Government eventually incarcerated at least eleven thousand ethnic Germans, almost all of whom were German nationals.

tant[12].

As far as the public knew, and notwithstanding the actions that were about to be taken against Japanese Americans, nobody was planning to go after large numbers of white American Protestants[13]. After all, in Robert's words, that "wasn't the American way."[14]

---

12. On his father's side, one of Robert's ancestors had served in the Continental Navy as first mate to Joshua Barney during America's War of Independence. In the course of the War, he was captured by the British, and was held as a Prisoner of War during the period when the Treaty of Paris was being negotiated with the British. See "The Boy Captain" (Seton Publishing, March, 2012).

13. In fact, the original plan drafted by the Government's Western Defense Command proposed rounding up Italians and Germans as well as Japanese Americans, but the Secretary of War, Henry Stimson, killed the idea, apparently because he thought the American public would not support the forced relocation of Americans of European descent.

14. It turns out that there was precedent for what happened to Japanese Americans – though it was not grounded on race. At the conclusion of the American Revolution, large numbers of British loyalists were imprisoned, and their property confiscated, until a formal peace treaty was signed by representatives of the United Kingdom.

4 - *Internment*

Decades later, the public learned that in the hours immediately following the attack on Pearl Harbor, the Federal Bureau of Investigation secretly rounded up more than a thousand Japanese Americans, mostly community and religious leaders, and incarcerated them in secret facilities located in North Dakota, New Mexico and Montana.

Many of these people, none of whom had committed any crime, would be prevented from contacting family or friends, and would be interned without any explanation until after the War had ended.

False allegations of widespread sabotage were circulated by Government Officials, and as a result, rumors were rampant in California and elsewhere on the mainland that Japanese Americans were prepared to support Japan in its war against the United States.

To make matters worse, many Americans believed that Japanese Americans living in the coastal regions of Washington, Oregon and California (where most Japanese Americans were living at the time) were actual spies who had been recruited by the Government of

Japan and its foreign agents[15].

Given these circumstances, it was hardly a surprise when, on February 19, 1942, President Franklin Roosevelt issued Executive Order 9066, one of the most shameful acts by any President of the United States in the history of the Republic.

Japanese Americans were not explicitly named in the order, but it was clear from the beginning that they were the people being targeted by the President.

What the Order did say was that various unnamed people who lived in coastal areas of the West Coast could and would be forcibly taken from their homes in those areas (the so-called "exclusion zones"), most of which were in California and the western portions of Arizona, Washington, and Oregon). They could be taken "for any reason" whatsoever, without any notice of charges, trial, or any other form of legal due process.

And they would be forcibly relocated to "secure facili-

---

15. Years later the Jimmy Carter Administration organized the "Commission on Wartime Relocation" to determine whether any Americans of Japanese Ancestry actually committed acts of espionage or sabotage. They determined that no such acts ever took place, and that the detention of Japanese Americans was the product of "race prejudice, war hysteria, and a failure of political leadership." Thereafter, Ronald Reagan signed the Civil Liberties Act, in which the Federal Government issued a series of apologies to every Japanese-American interned during the War, and paid $20,000 in compensation to each surviving internee.

ties" that were then being constructed by Government contractors[16].

Subsequent orders issued to the public by Lt. General John L. DeWitt, who was tasked with running the Western Defense Command, explicitly identified the targets of Executive Order 9066 as "anyone of Japanese ancestry." Shortly thereafter, the government moved to identify and require the registration of all persons of Japanese ancestry. It also put registrants on notice that they were barred from moving from their current locations[17], and it advised them that they would soon be

---

16. The United States Supreme Court, which is supposed to be a protector of our civil rights, upheld convictions of three Japanese Americans who supposedly violated regulations issued pursuant to Executive Order 9066: Minoru Yasui, Gordon Hirabayashi and Fred Korematsu. All three convictions were eventually reversed by the 9th Circuit Court of Appeals on the basis of newly- discovered evidence. The relocation order itself was not reversed until December 18,1944, when a unanimous Supreme Court held that the government could not continue to detain a citizen who was "concededly loyal" to the United States. See Ex Parte Mitsueye Endo, 323 US 283 (1944).

17. No wholesale action was ever announced against most of the 160,000 Japanese Americans living in Hawaii. The reason for that inaction was apparently grounded on the notion that there were so many Japanese Americans living in that small State that it would be impossible to relocate all of them. Nonetheless, according to Government figures, approximately 1,000 Japanese Americans living in Hawaii were, in fact, interned against their will.

forcibly moved to "secure locations."[18]

In the aftermath of these announcements, somewhere between 110,000 and 120,000 persons of Japanese Ancestry, half of whom were children, and sixty percent of whom were born in the United States – and as such were American citizens – were deprived of their basic constitutional rights without any due process whatsoever[19].

It was later announced that most of those who were relocated would be placed in what were then called, euphemistically, "wartime communities," that were located in remote areas scattered throughout the west coast of the United States.

Ninety percent of the permanent internment camps set up by the Government were run by the Federal War Relocation Authority (the WRA), and <u>all</u> of the internees in those camps were Japanese Americans.

Shockingly, the relocation centers were not simply "wartime communities", as described in WRA propaganda, but were concentration camps, purely and

---

18. Incredibly, there were several instances where Japanese American children who had been adopted by Caucasian parents were jerked out of school, taken from their adoptive mothers and fathers, and shipped off to relocation centers.

19. Under the Fourteenth Amendment of the United States Constitution, anyone born in the United States is automatically an American citizen. See also 18 USC section 1401, which elaborates on and reinforces the Constitutional provision.

simply.

Multiple families were assigned to small living quarters, and the camps themselves were surrounded by barbed wire and watchtowers. In several camps, orphans of Japanese ancestry were housed in miniature "orphanages" that were set up in "secure" areas, allegedly for the protection of the young internees.

Guards armed with automatic weapons made sure that internees stayed inside the strict confines of the camps, and there were numerous reports of shootings that occurred when internees dared to step outside the enclosures that surrounded them.

As an immediate consequence of Executive Order 9066, Raymond and his family were forced to register with the United States Army. And within days after that, they were informed that sometime that week they would be given forty-eight hours' notice that they would be forcibly relocated to an unspecified location.

In the meantime, their bank accounts were frozen, and they were instructed that when they were transported they would be limited to a single bag for their personal possessions, and that they would not be allowed to take radios or cameras with them.

5 - *Entrusting Assets*

Alarmed by the injustice that was about to be imposed on his friends, Robert loaded up many personal items belonging to the Ishimatsu family into a pickup truck, and he drove them over the Santa Cruz Mountains and stored them at his grandparent's ranch in Santa Cruz. Unfortunately, there was nothing he could do in the short time that was available to protect the Ishimatsu ranch house, or the vehicles, tractors and other machinery that they used to conduct their farming business[20].

When Robert dropped off the Ishimatsu's personal property in Santa Cruz, his grandfather questioned him about it. "Why are you helping them, Robert? Don't you think you might get in trouble with the Government?"

"Frankly, Grandpa, what happened to Mr. Ishi could

---

20. One of the items that Robert moved to Santa Cruz was a large console radio with short wave and regular broadcast bands that was a prized possession of the Ishimatsu family. Ironically, during the period the Ishimatsus were interned, Robert's grandparents used that radio to listen to addresses by President Roosevelt and other Government officials in which they communicated with American citizens on the progress of the War.

have happened to you and Grandma. You were both born in Germany, and there are people in this Country who think that Germans like you should be rounded up, just the same as Japanese."

"But Robert, we love this Country. And I have lived here for almost eighty years."[21]

"But that's the whole point, Grandpa. Raymond's family has been in America as long as you have, and they love America, too. To round them up, and treat them like criminals, betrays every principle Americans have always stood for."

That night, when Robert returned to the Ishimatsu ranch he was met by Raymond's sister, Carol. "Robert," she told him, "It's official. We are being shipped out of town by train in five days!"

The next day, Mr. Ishi received word that an emergency meeting of family heads of Santa Clara County's large Japanese community had been called for later that day at the San Jose Civic Auditorium.

Of course Mr. Ishi, as did most of his neighbors, attended the meeting which lasted several hours.

The principal speaker at the meeting was a gentleman by the name of Amadeo ("A. P.") Giannini, who was at the time the president and founder of what was origi-

---

21. Fred Pracht had come to the United States as a young child with his parents in 1861. According to Fred, his father's motive for leaving Germany and immigrating to the United States was to avoid being drafted into the Prussian Army.

nally known in San Jose as the Bank of Italy.

That Bank was one of the first financial institutions in the United States that marketed itself to lower and middle class Americans – many of whom were immigrants – and by the 1940s the Bank (which had by then changed its name) had already established a reputation for itself as the "bank you can trust."

As Mr. Giannini began to speak, his sound system failed, so he left the stage at the front of the auditorium and walked into the middle of the audience, which consisted of more than two thousand people, and spoke without a microphone.

"I know that many of you are recent immigrants, or the sons of recent immigrants, and yet I speak to you in English, because I know that learning English, and adopting the ways of this Country, is important to all of you. I, too, am the son of immigrants, and I know how important it was to my parents to assimilate the customs and values of the United States, and to learn the English language. Those values," he continued, "include the right to be treated equally and fairly under the law, and they have been betrayed by General Order 9066."

At this he received a standing ovation.

And he continued with what appeared to be great emotion on his part. "Because President Roosevelt and General DeWitt have announced that you will be relocated in a matter of days, and because they have given you little or no time to dispose of your assets, you stand to lose your homes, your businesses, and whatever real property you can't fit into a single bag. Stated plainly, you stand to lose virtually all of your earthly possessions. And this is wrong. But I am willing to do something about it. In a few minutes I will be distributing what are called 'Trust Agreements,' one to each of you for your families. If you sign those Trust Agreements, and I hope you will, you will be turning all of your possessions, including your land, over to the Bank. For its part, the Bank and I personally promise to take care of your property until the end of the War, and to return your possessions to you at that time."

At first Mr. Giannini's proposal was met with silence.

"What choice do we have?" shouted a man who was sitting next to Mr. Ishi. And "How do we know you will keep your word?" shouted another man, Hideo Sugiyama, who was one of Mr. Ishi's neighbors in Cupertino.

By this time, Mr. Giannini was covered with sweat, and his voice was fading. He responded, "Because I am an American, and I believe in the rights that are imbedded in our Constitution."

"Why don't you tell that to President Roosevelt?" shouted another neighbor. "The President doesn't care about the Constitution. Look what's happening to us!"

Mr. Giannini simply shook his head, and there was another long silence.

Finally, Mr. Ishi stepped forward. "I'll sign your Trust Agreement," he said, "on behalf of myself and my family. But," he said, pointing his finger at Mr. Giannini, "God help you if you don't keep your word."

Then one by one, virtually every man in the auditorium signed one of the Trust Agreements.

Suffice it to say that the Ishimatsu family was soon in a railway car on its way to an internment camp, and except for the personal property Robert had stored for them in Santa Cruz, virtually all of their possessions were in the hands of an American Bank.

On the face of it, the Bank could now do one of two things: it could breach its promises and unjustly enrich itself with millions of dollars rightfully belonging to more than a two thousand interned Japanese Americans; or it could act as an honest fiduciary and assure that the assets of the internees, and the income from those assets, was preserved and turned over to the families who entrusted them to the Bank.

Without ruining the story of what eventually happened to the Trust Agreements, be assured that you will find out at the end of this book in Chapter 23. So stay tuned.

6 - Robert Enlists

Once the United States had formally declared War against Japan, Robert felt he had no choice but to enlist in the army. His father had urged him to ask for a deferment so that he could finish his up his doctoral degree, and then enlist as an officer.[22]

But Robert refused. He told his father that "everybody" was signing up, and that it would be unpatriotic to evade the draft. But to please his father, Robert formally applied for a commission with the Navy.

It turned out that Robert's draft board had other plans in mind. In February of 1942, Robert was ordered to appear for a medical examination at the Induction Center in downtown Oakland, California.

The so-called "examination" was cursory at best.

---

22. Robert's father was a graduate engineer from Berkeley whose brother was killed in World War I. During the Great Depression he was fortunate enough to find work as a surveyor for the State of California, and he held that job from the early 1930s until he died in the early 1950s.

Indeed, almost nobody who had appeared at the Induction Center was rejected, although it seemed to Robert that there were a large number of prospective recruits who had physical limitations that almost certainly would have precluded them from serving their country, at least during the period which preceded Pearl Harbor.

Some individuals with advanced degrees, including several men Robert recognized as his classmates in graduate school at the University of California, were shuttled off to separate tables, apparently so they could be evaluated for possible commissions in one of the armed services[23].

But for some reason, Robert was not flagged for any special consideration, and he found himself thrown together with hundreds of other young men who would soon be designated as privates, and shipped to various locations across the Country for basic training.

---

23. Many months later, while he was serving as an enlisted man in New Guinea, Robert received a letter which was forwarded to him by his parents. The letter advised him that he had been selected for Officer Training in California, and that he should present himself for registration at the Treasure Island Naval Base one week later. Needless to say, the presentation date had long since passed when Robert received it, and he was never commissioned as an officer.

7 - Santa Anita Racetrack

In March of 1942, when the final order came to relocate Japanese Americans living in the San Francisco Bay Area, including San Jose, the Ishimatsu family was taken by train to the Santa Anita Racetrack in Southern California. There the internees were held in what they were told was "temporary housing" until permanent facilities were completed.

The Racetrack housing consisted primarily of dormitories that were built in horse stalls. None of these had been properly cleaned, and they smelled of manure.

Additional housing was built in a parking lot alongside the horse stalls, but these dormitories reeked of tar paper which covered the asphalt under the housing, and sweated in the hot climate of Los Angeles.

The internees were told they would be assigned "community maintenance work," all of which was to be performed within the racetrack. The racetrack proper was surrounded by barbed wire. And the work performed by the internees consisted of sewing camouflage netting that would cover open areas of the racetrack.

Each internee was assigned a single "army cot" with a straw "tick," and one blanket. The internees were supposed to supply their own toiletries, eating utensils and linens, but many such items were unavailable because of the requirement that they bring all their belongings in a single bag.

Anyone who wanted to use a toilet, or take a shower, or eat a meal at various makeshift "mess halls," had to stand in long lines.

In other words, life at Santa Anita was uncomfortable, smelly, and unpleasant in every way imaginable. Not surprisingly, in early August of 1942 a riot broke out as a result of overcrowding and the lack of decent food.

In the fall of 1942, word was sent out that the racetrack would soon be returned to its original use, and the internees would be taken by train and buses to a new facility at Manzanar, California, which few had ever heard of, and even fewer had ever seen. Nobody knew what to expect.

8 - Basic Training

Once he had filled out his enlistment papers, Robert expected to be sent to Fort Benning, Georgia, the self-proclaimed "Home of the Infantry" since 1909. But that didn't happen. Instead, he was sent to the Army's School of Medicine in Abilene, Texas. There he attended class with other recruits who were being trained as combat medics.

Almost half a century later, Robert described the experience in a journal he wrote for his children and grandchildren. "I wouldn't say the country around Abilene was completely barren – it would probably support one cow if you had two hundred acres."

As bleak as life was in Texas, it was there that he met many recruits with whom he engaged in discussions about the issues of the day. In the course of these discussions, he learned firsthand about the views average Americans held about matters that concerned him. Primary among these, of course, was the forced relocation of innocent Japanese Americans into concentration camps.

To his amazement, virtually everybody he talked to

expressed anxiety about the patriotism of those Americans, and as much as he tried, he was unable to convince any of his fellow recruits about the injustice worked upon Japanese American people that he knew were as thoughtful, gracious, and patriotic as any other American – if not more so.

Analogies he drew to German Americans or to Italian Americans fell on deaf ears, and Robert quickly learned that the disgraceful round up and internment of Japanese Americans was a topic that was best avoided[24]. This was discouraging, of course, but at the end of the day he concluded there was nothing he could do about it.

Once he and his fellow recruits completed their training as medics, virtually all of his classmates received orders that dispatched them to the European theater.

The War against Germany had started badly for the United States, and although the Allies had scored some military victories in North Africa, the going was slow, and the President had decided to move large numbers of his newest troops to join an Allied force that would invade Europe from the south.

Robert expected to join these men. But that never happened. Instead, he was told he would remain in Abi-

---

24. It turns out that many prominent Americans had racist views that paralleled those that spawned Executive Order 9066. Among these were California Attorney General (and eventual Chief Justice) Earl Warren, California Governor Culbert Olson, and, of course, President Franklin Roosevelt.

lene, and would be assigned a permanent position working as an assistant for one of the physicians who ran a small laboratory that was located within the Abilene Medical School.

At first, Robert was surprised, and a little miffed, by his new assignment. But he learned later that the physician who would be his boss, Captain Al Gagne, had selected him to be his assistant because of the graduate work Robert had done on infectious diseases while studying at the University of California.

Indeed, as will be seen below, Robert's expertise on that subject would affect him throughout the remainder of the War. And his relationship with Captain Gagne would not only affect his wartime service, but would dramatically affect the rest of his life.

9 - *Manzanar*

At the start of World War II, Manzanar was a near ghost town located at the foot of the Sierra Nevada Mountains in a cold, dusty area approximately two hundred miles north of Los Angeles. It was once home to Native Americans, but it had been abandoned by them in the mid-1800s, and by almost everyone else by the early 1900s. It was there that the Government established one of the first and the largest internment Camp for the incarceration of Japanese Americans.

It was fully operational from March of 1942 until November of 1945.

The Camp was located on a parcel of more than 6,000 acres, but the developed area was far smaller, i.e., approximately 500 acres surrounded by barbed wire and eight watch towers.

The desert area around the Camp was bleak and barren, and the Camp's elevation, at approximately 4,000 feet, assured that the internees would be exposed to extreme heat in the summer, and extreme cold in the winter.

Individual housing units erected at the camp were

small, and offered scant protection against the elements, and many internees became sick and even died because of dust and other climatic conditions there.

Bathrooms were nothing more than "communal latrines" which afforded no privacy whatsoever.

Most of the thirty-six "group housing units" were broken up into twenty-by-twenty-five foot spaces, with one space allotted to each family, and with no ceilings or partitions.

All meals were taken at large communal mess halls offering food that usually consisted of rice and vegetables, and seldom included meat or other protein of any kind.

And there were ridiculously long lines not only for food, but for the communal latrines, and for use of the laundry.

Daily life at Manzanar was accompanied by almost constant indignities. Internees were referred to as "Jap," and not by their names, and the guards, who controlled nearly every aspect of camp life, would routinely insult the internees for such "offenses" as walking "too slow" in bussing their empty food trays, or for talking "too loud" during communal meals, or for speaking "out of turn" by complaining that their food was tainted, too hot, or too cold.

There was an incident when a guard actually spit into a cauldron of soup, and that outrage, together with another incident in which an elderly internee was swatted by the butt of a guard's rifle for standing too close to the barbed wire fence that circled the camp, led to a demonstration that occurred in December of 1942.

The demonstration was organized by community leaders selected by the internees during clandestine meetings that were held in the mess halls during evening meals.

Mr. Ishi and his neighbor from Cupertino, Hideo Sugiyama, were among these community leaders. In planning the demonstration, its organizers made it clear to all participants that they should be polite and non-confrontational, but also firm in demanding that their basic demands should be met. Those demands, which were hardly controversial, boiled down to requests for better food, including meat, for shorter lines, for access to daily newspapers, and for regular meetings between internee representatives and the Camp's management.

But as the demonstration began, guards saw it as a threat, and treated it as though it was an armed insurrection.

Machine guns were fired over the heads of marchers, and the demonstration turned into a riot.

By the time order was restored, seventeen internees had been injured, including three children who had been hit by stray bullets.

But the demonstration resulted in some improvements. Sunday editions of the *Los Angeles Times* (redacted by the Camp's management) were delivered on a weekly basis, and internees were allowed to grow gardens of their own, and to keep chickens in small coops that were installed next to the communal meal halls.

Most importantly, the Camp's Commander, Major Frank Butler, agreed that he would meet with internee representatives on a regular basis. These representatives included both Mr. Ishi and Hideo Sugiyama.

<u>*10 - Life in Abilene*</u>

After finishing his training as a medic, Robert had been eager to get into combat. At that point he had never seen combat, of course, and the fact that his uncle had been killed while fighting the Germans in World War I, should have forewarned him that War is frightening. But he really didn't see it that way. In his mind, at least at the outset, the whole pageant of joining the military and being posted to some exotic far off land was something of an adventure.

So when he learned that his first assignment would involve his working in a laboratory at the medical school in Abilene, he was somewhat disappointed.

But it was there that he made his first real friend in the Army. This was his boss, Captain Al Gagne, a man only slightly older than Robert, who had been born and raised in Massachusetts.

"Doctor Al," as everyone called him, was a big man – slightly more than six feet five inches tall – loud and boisterous. He was athletic and a wonderful story teller, and he was so extroverted that he would immediately take over any conversation he was involved in. His favorite stories almost always related to his native Boston, where he had been raised in a Catholic household with nine siblings.

But Doctor Al had another trait that Robert found reassuring: he shared Robert's disgust for the treatment of Japanese Americans who were being interned in California and elsewhere.

Doctor Al had spent his undergraduate years at Boston College, and by the time the War started, he had graduated from Harvard School of Medicine, and he was searching for a suitable residency. But the Army being the Army he was denied a residency, and instead, after he received a commission as Captain, he, too, was sent to Abilene.

In the spring of 1942, he was assigned to command the same lab where Robert would soon be working, and it was there that the two men developed a lifelong friendship.

They had a mutual interest in Entomology and Epidemiology, but they also shared other interests, including sports in general, and tennis in particular. Robert had excelled at tennis while he was a student at the University of California, and so it was not surprising that at the end of any given work day in Abilene, Doctor Al and Robert could usually be found at one of Base's dusty clay tennis courts playing "doubles" with the Base Commander and his adjutant.

Professionally, Doctor Al and Robert worked well together, and they developed a reputation for the diagnosis and treatment of Malaria and other insect borne diseases. And not surprisingly, that reputation caught the attention of their military detailers.

Men with that talent were precisely what was needed in the Pacific theater, and to nobody's surprise, in the spring of 1943, Doctor Al was re-assigned to run an Australian laboratory testing for such diseases.

The laboratory had been set up in a small brewery located in Melbourne. It was owned by Tooth & Company and affiliated with the much larger Kent Brewery in New South Wales that had been founded in 1835.

As soon as he received his new assignment, Doctor Al requested that Robert be assigned to the same laboratory. But he wasn't. Instead, Robert, who was now a "Staff Sergeant," was told that he would soon be sent to a different location. But he wasn't told where it would be.

In the twelve months that followed, Doctor Al enjoyed the life of a physician working in a brewery, far from any war zone. He had access to concerts and the theater, and he was a regular patron at a nearby movie theater.

But he missed his friend Robert, and he made several more requests to locate Robert, and have him transferred to Melbourne, all to no avail.

11 - Raymond Enlists

After spending the better part of a year in internment, Raymond could easily have been bitter. But he wasn't. When his family was initially sent to the Santa Anita Race Track, he was disappointed that his idealistic vision of America had been shattered.

But he told his family that he understood the frustration felt by many Americans who were distrustful of Asian-Americans[25].

As time wore on, and the Ishimatsu family was moved to Manzanar, he reconciled himself to life in an internment camp, and he busied himself writing a memoir which he thought he might try to publish once the War was over.

---

25. In 1909, California law was amended to add persons of Japanese ancestry to a list of "undesirable" marriage partners for white persons. And in 1931, a new California statute prohibited outright any marriage between persons of Caucasian and Asian races. These so-called "miscegenation" laws passed by various States were ultimately declared unconstitutional by the United States Supreme Court in <u>Loving vs. Virginia</u>, 388 US 1 (1967).

His sister Carol and his mother busied themselves cutting the hair of older women at the Camp, and Mr. Ishi began working on a cook book in which he shared "secret" recipes he had learned from his father and grandfather.

"Maybe I can open a restaurant after the war," Mr. Ishi announced one night, and everyone nodded enthusiastically. But if the truth be told, his family privately assumed that at the end of the War all of their property would be gone, and that the family would have to start life from scratch if, and when, they were freed from the Camp.

When Raymond first learned in early 1943 that the Army had dropped its ban on Japanese American enlistments, and was establishing a new regiment which would consist solely of Japanese Americans, he told his family that he might want to sign up.

His sister, Carol, chided him at first, arguing that it was foolish to risk your life for a country that didn't respect you or your heritage.

But Raymond's mind was made up.

His decision was prompted in large part by a young woman whom he had known when he was living in Cupertino, and who was now with her family in Manzanar, Dorothy Sugiyama. Dorothy's father, Hideo, was one of the organizers of the demonstration that had occurred in December of 1942, and was one of the representatives selected by the internees to meet with the Camp's Commander after the ensuing riot.

In their time at Manzanar, Raymond and Dorothy had grown quite close, and she was playing an increasingly important role in his life. She strongly encouraged Raymond, as well as her twin brother, Toshitada or "Tosh," to enlist for duty in Europe; it was Dorothy, more than anyone else, who convinced Raymond to serve his country in a military capacity.

In March of 1943 Raymond and Tosh both joined the 442nd regiment, an army unit manned solely by so called "Nisei," i.e., persons of Japanese descent who were born and educated in the United States, many of whom had been interned until they enlisted[26].

Owing to their graduate work, on April 1, 1943 Raymond and Tosh were both sworn in as second lieutenants, and they were shipped to a staging area that had been set up for the 442nd Regiment in New Jersey.

As with Raymond's friend, Robert, who was about to be shipped thousands of miles away from home, the lives of Raymond and Tosh were about to take dramatic new turns.

---

26. Ironically, in one of the most hypocritical statements ever made by an American leader, the same President Roosevelt who had issued Executive Order 9066 in 1942, had this to say when he issued the Executive Order that created the 442nd Regiment in 1943: "The principle on which this country was founded and by which it has always been governed is that Americanism is a matter of mind and heart; Americanism is not, and never was, a matter of race or ancestry."

12 - *New Guinea*

After leaving Abilene, Robert was in the dark about where he would be going next.

At first he was taken by train to Charleston, South Carolina. Then, a week later, he was taken by bus to Newport News, Virginia. There he boarded a troop ship with ten thousand other men.

After leaving port, Robert's ship steamed in an easterly direction, and everyone assumed they were headed for Europe. But after a day of sailing east, the ship suddenly turned south, and it ended up going through the Panama Canal.

When his ship emerged into the Pacific Ocean, it joined a convoy of nine other troop ships, and they maintained a course that "zigged and zagged," but mostly went southwest.

Five weeks later the convoy pulled into port at New Caledonia, a French Territory that is about seven hundred fifty miles east of Australia.

They remained in New Caledonia long enough to bring supplies on board, and then they steamed west to Brisbane, on the East Coast of Australia.

It was there that Robert learned that he had been assigned to head a ten-person "station hospital" at Mareeba, a small town in Northeastern Australia about forty miles west of the port city of Cairns on the Coral Sea.

It turned out that the station hospital was simply a training facility, and in short order Robert received a new assignment. He and the ten persons assigned to him would be shipped by air to New Guinea. There they would be sent to an advance medical unit known as Camp Theodore Roosevelt (named after the 26th President) at Nadzab, New Guinea, a nondescript town which was located several miles east of Lae, a major port city in Eastern Papua.

A dirt road connected Lae and Nadzab, but Japanese troops stationed along the coast north of Lae in Bukaua had captured portions of that road, and the few convoys that managed to drive between Nadzab and Lae came under heavy fire.

To make matters worse, a company of infantrymen that had originally been assigned to Camp Roosevelt had recently been deployed to an adjacent island. So the Camp was essentially defenseless, and except for an occasional convoy used to ferry fresh troops in, and take wounded troops out, virtually all supplies delivered to Camp Roosevelt had to be dropped by parachute.

Robert's assignment was to analyze blood samples taken from the few troops that were still attached to

Camp Roosevelt. Those troops were under almost constant fire, and were plagued by mosquitoes carrying malaria.

His work was grueling, and it was not unusual for Robert to work fifteen hours or more in a single day.

Robert caught malaria shortly after his arrival, but the disease was diagnosed almost immediately, and that fact and his early treatment limited the damage done to him. Nonetheless, he experienced weeks of shaking chills alternating with high fever, profuse sweating, and vomiting. And, of course, his recovery was complicated by the work he continued trying to perform for his fellow GI's.

Daily bombings by Japanese torpedo planes usually occurred late in the afternoon, just before dinner. The attacks were so predictable that most of the men were numbed to their occurrence. But a few men broke under the pressure, and had to be shipped back to the States and placed in mental hospitals.

One of the few diversions at Camp Roosevelt was a wild pig Robert had named Betty (after Betty Grable). He discovered Betty one morning as she was helping herself to sugary powder the mess hall had used to create makeshift ice cream. Over the next few days, Robert mixed more of the powder with clean water from a nearby creek, and he fed it to Betty at the end of each work day. From that time forward, and to the amusement of all hands, wherever Robert went, Betty was sure to follow.

At some point somebody took a photograph of Betty and sent it to *Stars and Stripes*, a semi-official daily newspaper for GI's in the field, that was published inside the Department of Defense, and was distributed to troops at various theaters throughout the War.

Incredibly, Betty's picture was placed on the front page of the newspaper. This meant two things. First, Robert's unit now had an official mascot. But more important (at least for Betty), it meant that any plans the Sergeant in charge of the Camp's Mess Hall might have to serve Betty as an hors d'oeuvre were put on permanent hold.

As it turned out, Robert was to have at least one other contact with *Stars and Stripes*.

After he had been in New Guinea for about six months, Robert wrote a letter to the newspaper, criticizing GI's who were constantly complaining about the Army's failure to improve life on the front lines. In his letter, which was published shortly after he submitted it for publication, Robert said: "Instead of grumbling about what the United States can do for you, how about focusing on what you can do for the United States."

Years later, when the War was over, and Robert was living in Sacramento, California, he heard John F. Kennedy use a similar admonition in his first speech as President of the United States[27]. Upon hearing that,

---

27. In his inaugural address on January 20, 1961, President Kennedy said: "Ask not what your country can do for you; ask what you can do for your country."

Robert complained that Kennedy had probably read his letter to *Stars and Stripes* while he was serving in the Western Pacific on PT-109, and he stole his idea.

I won't comment on who stole what from whom. Suffice it to say that from the author's research, similar sentiments were expressed as far back as during revolutionary times, and were uttered by many others, including George Washington.

In the spring of 1944, Robert's unit was informed by its commander, Colonel Ernest Conway, that Army intelligence had determined that Japanese troops were advancing on them from the northeast coast of Papua, and would very likely surround them in the coming seven to ten days.

There was no mention of evacuation. Instead, the men of Fort Roosevelt were ordered to destroy all government records, including code books, and to prepare for the possibility that they would be taken into custody as POWs of the Japanese who were advancing toward Nadzab.

For anyone not willing to become a POW, Colonel Conway promised that backpacks, pistols, and several pounds of K-rations would be prepared for anyone willing to "go it alone," and "fend for yourself."

The "fend for yourself" option was given to Robert's unit at a mess hall meeting of all the men, and Colonel Conway asked for a show of hands by anyone who was interested. There was a long pause, and for a moment it appeared that nobody would volunteer.

But one man finally raised his hand. It was Robert.

According to him, "I guess I'm not cut out for life as a POW, Colonel, and I sure don't want to spend the rest of the War eating boiled rice."

So he prepared to set off on his own.

He carefully checked his backpack, and added antibiotics to the other essentials that had been packed for him by the Camp's medics.

He then waited for further word from Army intelligence.

On the morning of the day he was supposed to head into the jungle, he was surprised by a rare bombing run by Allied planes. The bombing was directed at Bukaua, which was uncomfortably close to Nadzab, and, as everyone knew, it was almost certainly the source of the "surrounding force" that was headed for Camp Roosevelt.

When the bombing stopped, Robert was approached by Colonel Conway, and asked if he was sure that he still wanted to fend for himself. Robert indicated that he was "good to go," and he shook hands with the Colonel. He picked up his back pack, loaded his pistol, and headed into the jungle.

But then the unexpected happened.

He noticed, almost immediately, that he had been joined by a sidekick that he hadn't planned on. It was his pet pig, Betty.

At first he tried to shoo Betty away, but the pig couldn't

be moved. After several tries, Robert gave up. Instead, he fed her a piece of candy that had been loaded into his backpack. "If you can't beat them, you might as well join them," he mouthed to himself, and he headed toward a tall bluff that was about a mile to the northeast. He was well aware that Bukaua was dangerously close by, but he felt that it was more important to locate the advancing Japanese troops before he headed south toward Lae. In his mind, the view from the bluff would give him a chance to assess the situation before he committed to a route to safety.

It was slow going as he moved through the heavy brush of the jungle, but he was eager to reach the bluff before dark, figuring that he could work out a specific plan after he reached the top.

The sun began to set as Robert reached the bluff, and he climbed to the top in time to see the lights from Lae to the south and Bukaua to the east.

Betty was still at his side, of course, and he fed her additional pieces of candy that he took from his backpack. She snorted with glee as she chewed the candy, and Robert smiled broadly as she finished one piece and then another.

"At this rate," Robert thought, "Betty will be better fed than me."

He scanned the horizon, looking for signs of Japanese forces, but at first he couldn't locate anything looking like an enemy camp.

He was about to give up his search when he saw what

looked like Allied bombers approaching from the south. As the bombers got closer, he could see artillery being fired at them from a coastal area east of the bluff, very near the place where thought he had seen the lights of Bukaua. This was a revelation, because he now knew exactly where the Japanese forces were advancing.

As it turned out, the bombing run lasted far longer than he had expected, and after about thirty minutes he noticed that fewer and fewer artillery shells were being shot at the Allied bombers. And another fifteen minutes later, the artillery shells had stopped altogether.

This was totally unexpected, and Robert decided that before he headed south toward Lae he would first head approximately one mile north to the coast of Papua, and then proceed east along the shoreline and try to determine what the Japanese were up to.

At five o'clock in the morning, Robert climbed down the bluff, and he and Betty headed north through the jungle. When they reached the northern shore of Papua, they followed the beach east toward Bukaua.

And after walking east for another hour or so, they reached a narrow strip of beach from which he could see something amazing. There were at least a dozen landing crafts, each flying a Japanese flag, that were being loaded from the shore with guns, vehicles, and troops. Clearly, the Japanese were abandoning Bukaua.

Robert could hardly believe his eyes, but he decided it was time to head west, and rejoin his Unit at Camp Roosevelt.

This he did, and twenty-four hours later he and Betty were enjoying candy and roast beef in the Camp Roosevelt mess hall.

Colonel Conway was delirious with joy when he learned that the Japanese had abandoned Bukaua. For now, at least, nobody would be taken prisoner, and he and his Unit could continue their work in support of the infantry unit that was expected to return to Camp Roosevelt within the week.

13 - Italy

Notwithstanding the weekly delivery of the redacted Sunday edition of the *Los Angeles Times,* information about the War in Europe (much less the War in the Pacific) had been kept from the internees at Manzanar. But after joining the 442nd, Raymond and Tosh were quickly brought up to speed on the status of the fighting.

Allied forces in Europe were poised to attack the Germans from the south, and the plan was to enter Italy with units staged in Sicily and Naples.

Nobody was quite sure how the Nisei troops would commend themselves, but the world was soon to discover that the 442nd was a force like no other. While taking horrific losses in the field[28], the Nisei were an awesome force, striking fear in anyone who opposed them.

---

28. Some commentators believe that over the course of the War, the 442nd suffered one of the highest rates of casualties of any Allied regiment in the European theater. Certainly, they were one of the most decorated of any American unit.

Indeed, by the time they reached German troops in Monte Cassino, which other Allied forces had been unable to defeat, the German forces there were so terrorized by the mere appearance of the Nisei that many positions were simply abandoned by hardened Nazi forces who had no stomach for combat against the 442nd.

But it was here that Raymond and Tosh Sugiyama first encountered elite German troops who were hand-picked by the *SS Wehrmacht* to hold what had previously been a deteriorating line of defense in Central Italy.

Raymond and Tosh had only been in Europe for a few months, but they had already been identified by their Company Commander as fearless officers who would willingly take on any assignment that others might find impossibly difficult.

When their unit first approached a major blockade just south of Monte Cassino, their Commander informed them that the Allied push was now hopelessly stalled, and that there was no way our troops would be able to press through the *SS Wehrmacht* unit commanded by the legendary Field Marshal Albert Kesselring.

Raymond and Tosh had encountered Kesselring once before, when their unit first landed in Sicily. Kesselring had withdrawn shortly thereafter, but not before delivering devastating losses on the advancing units of the 442nd led by Raymond and Tosh's commander, Colonel Sherman Akai.

Colonel Akai had been killed in that engagement, and

since he, Tosh, and Raymond had all been close, Raymond and Tosh wanted to avenge the loss of their friend and mentor.

Raymond told Akai's successor, Colonel Ronald Sato, that he and Tosh had a plan to break through Field Marshal Kesselring's lines. Colonel Sato was new to combat, but he knew Kesselring's forces were strong, and he was eager to learn what Raymond and Tosh had in mind. What they envisioned was a tactic they said they had learned while studying history at San Jose High School. Specifically, they wanted to duplicate the tactics used by the Greeks against the Persians in 480 B.C. (Thermopylae), and more recently by the Sioux against the Seventh Cavalry in 1876 (the Little Big Horn).

The basics of the tactic are that the attacking force starts in a solid lateral flank, and then falls back in the center of its line, giving the defenders the false impression that the attackers have lost heart, and are retreating. But they are not retreating, but they are enticing the enemy to enter the middle of their line in such a way as to allow them to become surrounded.

After hearing Raymond and Tosh explain the tactic, Colonel Sato told them he would give it a try.

As promised, the next morning Raymond and Tosh lined up at each end of their troops in a straight lateral line at the bottom of a tall hill held by the *SS Wehrmacht*. The troops ran up the Hill toward Kesselring's line, and then fell back in the middle third of their line, and seemed to "wither" in their charge. As predicted, the

Germans thought the Americans were retreating, and charged into the middle of the line. But Tosh's and Raymond's troops were ready. As the Germans charged down the hill, Tosh and Raymond's men circled around them, and then mowed them down with a combination of flamethrowers and hand grenades that stunned the Germans and sent them into a panic.

Colonel Sato, who was watching the battle from the bottom of the hill, smiled at the disarray displayed by Kesselring's men. He said to his adjutant, who was by his side, that Tosh and Raymond should get a medal for this. And they did. A month later Raymond and Tosh were both promoted to first lieutenant and awarded the Silver Star for their actions against Kesselring's forces.

*   *   *   *   *

In early 1944, Raymond and Tosh's unit had joined forces with other Nisei units of the 442nd (which included a young officer named Daniel Inouye, who would later become the first Japanese American to serve in the United States Senate), and they participated in what would later be called the "Rome-Arno Campaign."

The Rome-Arno Campaign was an effort by the Allies to follow up on victories over the Germans in Central Italy by moving north to capture ports on the east and west sides of northern Italy.

Raymond and Tosh's unit, which was still under the command of Colonel Sato, was given the task of capturing the port city of Livorno (which is on the western coast of Tuscany), and then move north to the Arno River where it flows west from Florence through Pisa, and into the Tyrrhenian Sea.

From a tactical standpoint, German forces were tired, and were suffering from losses experienced in Central Italy and in the capture of Rome. But the Allied forces were also tired, and they had been drained of troops who were being readied for the assault on Normandy, which was scheduled for June.

Raymond and Tosh's unit was buoyed by the apparent weakness of the German troops, who were still under the command of Field Marshal Kesselring, the man they had defeated at Monte Cassino.

Unfortunately, the German troops defending Livorno turned out to be far stronger than anyone had predicted. Adolph Hitler had ordered Kesselring to defend Livorno at "all costs," and Kesselring had persuaded Hitler that he could do so, even if his rival, Irwin Rommel, were moved to France to fortify that Country against the long-expected Allied invasion from England.

When the 442nd reached Livorno, it was sent northwest to the port itself, which was heavily protected by German artillery. The Allies had artillery of their own, of course, but for more than a week there was a virtual standoff.

Finally, the Allies decided to execute a plan in which they would invade the Port of Livorno under cover of darkness, with troops attacking from the north and south.

When the day came for the invasion, Colonel Sato's troops moved quickly and silently, and might well have surprised the defending Germans but for a series of booby-traps and land mines that had been distributed around the perimeter of the Port in anticipation of a surprise attack.

One of the first to set off a trip wire was Colonel Sato, who was badly injured by the resulting explosion. He lost his left arm at the scene, and had to be evacuated to Rome for emergency treatment.

Shocked at the loss of his Commander, Colonel Sato's second in command, Colonel William Takata, immediately took over command, and he signaled his troops to pull back so they could consider a new plan of attack. The troops immediately pulled back, and Colonel Takata asked Tosh and Raymond what they thought should be done. They informed him that their two units should be combined into a single force, and that they would personally lead that force into the Port through the main gates of the facility.

Colonel Takata agreed, and Tosh and Raymond lined their troops up for a frontal assault on the gates.

Raymond and Tosh's combined unit had been joined temporarily by a company that was not a part of the 442nd, but consisted of "fresh" troops from the Army's Third Brigade, which had just arrived in Italy from California. Raymond recognized at least one of the regulars as an Italian American kid he had gone to school with in San Jose, Joe Brillo.

Brillo, who was a "jock" in high school, was the nephew of a guard at Manzanar, and as Tosh and Raymond led the charge toward the gates to the Port, Brillo shouted to them that he was proud to be fighting alongside the 442nd.

As they breached the actual gates of the Port, Brillo was one of the first casualties. He was shot in the leg, and was bleeding profusely, so Raymond shouted to Tosh to "get help" for the man. But instead of calling for help, Tosh took it upon himself to pick up Brillo, lift him over his shoulder, and carry him toward a medic who was setting up I-V bottles just inside the gates.

It was then that Tosh heard a burst of machine gun bullets, apparently fired by a German Guard who had been set up on the wall that encircled the Port. It was the last sound that Tosh would hear.

Looking back, Raymond saw that his friend had been hit, but he was at the head of his troops, and was under heavy fire, so he was forced to continue moving forward.

As they advanced, casualties were increasing. German land mines were still exploding, and for a time Raymond was tempted to fall back. But he refused to do so, and the tide of battle eventually turned in his favor.

Raymond himself blacked out briefly when a shell exploded next to a German artillery piece that had been booby-trapped with explosives. But he quickly regained consciousness, and when he looked back toward the gates of the port, he was buoyed to see that the American flag had been raised over the main entrance.

*   *   *   *   *

Once the fighting stopped, Raymond searched for Tosh, and he was unable to find him. Eventually he found Joe Brillo, alive but badly wounded, and it was Joe who told him that Tosh had been killed.

"I don't know what to say, Raymond, but that guy saved my life."

*   *   *   *   *

When he was told about his unit's victory, and he saw that the American flag was now flying over the Port, Colonel Takata told a pool reporter who was covering the fight that if Raymond and Tosh were still alive, they were almost certainly going to get medal for what they had done.

Two weeks later, Raymond was promoted to Major, and he was awarded his second Silver Star. Tosh also was awarded a Silver Star, but he received his posthumously.

For Raymond, his promotion and the honor of receiving a medal was completely overshadowed by the loss of his friend.

*   *   *   *   *

One month later, an honor guard appeared at the gates of Manzanar. At the head of the honor guard was a blond soldier wearing a dress blue uniform with a Purple Heart medal pinned to his chest. The soldier had trouble walking, but he kept himself upright by using steel crutches that he carried under each of his arms.

The soldier with the crutches was followed by six members of the 442nd who slowly marched in unison as they carried a flag-draped coffin holding the remains of Lieutenant Tosh Sugiyama.

As the honor guard passed through the gates and into the Camp, it was met by the Camp Commander, Major Butler, and by the members of the Sugiyama family.

It was also met by more than a thousand internees who had lined up on both sides of the narrow road that connected the front gates to a large auditorium that was normally used for general assemblies.

There was hardly a sound as the honor guard passed by, and it was almost as if time had stopped within the Camp.

When the honor guard reached the auditorium, the soldier with the crutches was met by a camp guard who embraced him, and then saluted him.

Inside the auditorium there was a small stage, and in the middle of the stage, someone had set up a lectern with a microphone and two large speakers to boost the sound from the microphone.

Hundreds of internees filed quietly into the auditorium, but the building quickly filled, and hundreds more had to stand outside as they waited for the remarks that would follow.

The first person to speak was Major Butler.

"Ladies and Gentlemen," he said, "This is a sad day for the family of Lieutenant Tosh Sugiyama, but it is also a sad day for the United States of America. Lieutenant Sugiyama, who was once an internee in this Camp, fought for this Country and ultimately gave his life for all of us. I cannot and will not pretend that the Sugiyama family has been treated fairly by this Country, but when this War is over, and our enemies are defeated, it will be because of men like Lieutenant Sugiyama, who paid the ultimate price to ensure all Americans the rights that were denied to him and his family."

The next person to speak was Joe Brillo, the blond soldier with the Purple Heart. He said, "Ladies and Gentlemen, you don't know me, and I don't know most of you. My uncle works as a guard at this camp, and he has impressed upon me that the Japanese Americans here in Manzanar are good, kind people, and love this Country as much as anybody. Today, many of you have sons who are fighting in Europe, and who are risking their lives to preserve America's values. One of those sons was Lieutenant Tosh Sugiyama, who gave his life under heavy fire as he carried me to safety." He began to cry, and added, "He didn't care whether I was an Italian American or any other kind of American that makes up this Country. He put his life on the line because I am a plain ol' American, same as him. Thank God for Lieutenant Sugiyama."

The final speaker was Hideo Sugiyama. "Many of you know me because of my role as a representative of the internees in this Camp. But that role is nothing compared to the role my son has played in this War. By joining the 442nd, as many of your sons have done, he has brought great credit on his family, and on all people of good will. My wife, who now wears a Gold Star, and I, and all of our family, will never be fully consoled for the death of our son and brother. But we will always be proud that he gave his life for others, and it is that memory that will live in our hearts for the rest of our lives."[29]

---

29. Lieutenant Tosh Sugiyama was later buried with full military honors at the San Francisco National Cemetery, which is near the Golden Gate Bridge in San Francisco, California.

14 - Australia

In June of 1944, Robert's commander, Colonel Conway, received a mysterious, unsigned cable from Allied headquarters which was addressed to "All Hands" in the Pacific Theater of Operations (the "PTO"). The cable stated that "The Allied Command in Melbourne is in urgent need of a person with an entomology background and experience in the analysis and diagnosis of tropical diseases. Ideally, the successful candidate would have done graduate work in epidemiology and/or malaria research from a major university such as the University of California at Berkeley."

In other words, the cable couldn't have zeroed in more precisely on anybody more than Staff Sergeant Robert Rose. And it was no mystery to Robert that the author of the cable could only have been generated by one person, Doctor Al Gagne.

For once the Army came up with a prompt solution to its "All Hands" request. Thirty days after the request was published, Robert was on a plane from New Guinea to Australia.

He was met at Melbourne's Essendon Aerodrome by Doctor Al, and was personally driven to the Tooth's Brewery to formally begin work with his old friend.

And in case you think I forgot to mention it, the Army Transport Service allowed Robert to bring Betty along as a "critical" part of the material he needed to fulfill his mission. Somehow the word "pig" on the airplane's manifest had been erased and changed to read "research animal."

So Betty was no longer a mere Army mascot. Instead, she was now, at least in the eyes of Uncle Sam, an Army research animal.

15 - *Kathleen Salmon*

Throughout most of the War in the Pacific, Australia was a country without Australian males. Notwithstanding Japanese actions against several towns in the northern part of the country, virtually all able-bodied Australian men had joined the military, and most of these fellows had been shipped to Europe to protect the mother country, Great Britain.

A few lucky Australians were sent to defend New Guinea, but very few men were assigned to protect Australia itself.

That is where the Americans came in. Early in the War, Australia's then prime minister[30], John Curtin, worked out an arrangement with the American Government under which American soldiers would be stationed in

---

30. Although there were five prime ministers during World War II. John Curtin of the Labor Party served in that capacity for most of the War, i.e. from October 7, 1941 until July 5, 1945. The other men who held that job were Robert Menzies (April 1939 to August 1941), Arthur McFadden (August 1941 to October 1941), Francis Forde (July 1945) and Ben Chifley (July 1945 to December 1949).

Australia, and would serve as the first line of defense against any overt military actions by the Japanese, whether by land or by sea.

Among the American soldiers who spent extended periods of time in Australia was General Douglas MacArthur, who escaped to Australia from the Philippines in March of 1942 after his troops were surrounded by Japanese forces on Corregidor, and who famously returned to Leyte in the Philippines in October of 1944.

Bereft of their own men, Australian women welcomed American GI's with open arms, and were eager to entertain them at USO facilities and other venues that were considered neighborly and patriotic.

One of these women was Kathleen Salmon, a young Australian actress.

Kathleen was descended from Irish Catholics who had settled in Australia in the early 1800s after being involuntarily transported there from Ireland for participating in rebellions against English rule[31].

Kathleen's family had flourished in Australia.

Her mother, who had started her professional life as an artist and a sometime actress, eventually became the first female judge in the Children's Court of the State of Victoria. Kathleen's father was the Director of the Melbourne Port, and her Uncle had been a Labor Party member of the Australian Parliament.

---

31. See "The Early Troubles" (Seton Publishing, October, 2011)

Her brother (who was then off fighting in New Guinea) had been a news correspondent on Australia's national radio network. And Kathleen's youngest sister, who was also an actress, had performed in numerous productions, and was a favorite of the critics.

Kathleen was well known for her work on soap operas, and for her roles in productions by the Therry Society[32], which performed original works as well as Shakespearian plays. She was also an accomplished athlete, having twice won Melbourne's Silver Spoon for excellence in tennis.

Kathleen's family was well connected with the movers and shakers of the Catholic Church. His Eminence, Archbishop Daniel Mannix, was a regular visitor at her home, and she was privileged to live in a household with full time help and a chauffeur.

By contrast, Robert, even before the War, was a farm boy who had studied science and agriculture, and who couldn't care less about high society or politics.

He had been born in the living room of his grandparents' home in Santa Cruz, and to a person, his relatives were of modest means.

---

32. One of the Therry Society's playwrights was novelist Morris West. Many of Mr. West's novels later became popular worldwide, and several became Hollywood movies: *The Shoes of the Fisherman* (1968), *The Devil's Advocate* (1977), *The Salamander* (1981), *The Naked Country* (1984), *The Second Victory* (1986), and *Cassidy* (1989).

All of Robert's extended family were Methodists, and most of them were suspicious of Catholics.

Nobody in his family (all of whom were Republicans) had ever entered politics – or even entertained the notion of running for office.

All told, it would have been safe to say that Robert and Kathleen were from different worlds. In fact, the only thing Robert seemed to have in common with Kathleen was that they were both accomplished at tennis.

But notwithstanding their dramatic differences in background, Bob and Kathleen were destined to be partners for life.

They met at a USO show that Kathleen's theater group put on for American troops in the late summer of 1944. And they clicked immediately. According to Kathleen's sister, Aileen, who was always a cheerleader for Kathleen, when Robert and Kathleen met it was love at first sight.

As stated by Robert in his Journal, many decades later: "I could not believe such a talented and gorgeous creature would have any interest in me. I asked her out, and was amazed that she agreed to go out with me. After a number of dates and meeting her family, I began to think I might have a chance for a permanent arrangement!"

But there was a problem. According to Robert, "Kathleen eventually let it be known that a non-Catholic was definitely not in her permanent plans."

At that time, Catholics and Protestants simply didn't mix. In fact, Catholics were strongly discouraged from attending Protestant religious services, and Catholics were forbidden to marry Protestants unless the Protestant agreed to "convert" to Catholicism.

And to make matters worse, Robert's family wasn't terribly fond of the Irish. To them, the Irish were too brash, were far too casual about matters of intimacy, and were basically untrustworthy.

Protestant funerals were dark, gloomy affairs, and contrasted greatly with Catholic wakes which were celebrations of life, heavily salted with alcohol.

Kathleen was so upset about her religious differences with Robert that she called off their relationship for a time. But the relationship resumed shortly thereafter when Robert began taking lessons in Catholicism from Pierre Roberge, a French Jesuit who was living in Australia.

And Robert was also encouraged by his Catholic friend, Doctor Al, who spent countless evenings with Robert discussing the Catholic faith, and encouraging him to pursue his relationship with Kathleen.

Compromises were ultimately made by both of them. In the words of Robert in his journal: "When I decided to take instruction in the Catholic faith it was not such a big jump as you might imagine, and Kathleen's approval didn't do any harm either. I was very fortunate finding Father Roberge to be my tutor. The man was a living saint, and I put him to the test...He was always available and intelligent, and able to answer questions that had bothered me for years! And patient. I mustn't forget how patient he was."

In March of 1945 Robert and Kathleen became engaged, and they scheduled their wedding for August 4, 1945.

16 - Dorothy Sugiyama

Tosh Sugiyama's twin sister, Dorothy, was born in 1924, the daughter of Hideo and Sumi Sugiyama, a prosperous couple who farmed apple orchards in the same neighborhood as the Ishimatsu family in rural Santa Clara County.

When World War II broke out, Dorothy was working as a receptionist at the Betsuin Buddhist Temple in downtown San Jose. The Temple, which had been designed by famed architect George Shimamoto, and built in San Jose's Japan Town (Nihonmachi) by the Nishiura Brothers in 1937, is located on Fifth Street, and is still a center of Japanese culture.

Japan Town had first developed alongside San Jose's Chinatown in the late 1890s as large numbers of Japanese migrated to the Santa Clara Valley because of its abundance of farm work.

Even before they were at Manzanar together, the Sugiyamas were social friends of the Ishimatsus, and because Raymond, Tosh, and Dorothy were all about the same age, and had gone to the same grammar school and high school, they were fast friends.

After President Roosevelt issued his infamous order 9066, Hideo Sugiyama joined Mr. Ishi in signing his assets over to the Bank at the same meeting attended by Mr. Ishi and presided over by A. P. Giannini at the San Jose Civic Auditorium.

And when the Ishimatsu family was relocated by the Government, and ultimately sent to Manzanar, the Sugiyamas were sent to the same "wartime community."

When Raymond and Dorothy's brother Tosh first started talking about joining the newly formed 442nd, Dorothy had supported the idea. In fact, it was Dorothy who finally won over Mr. Ishi in supporting Raymond's enlistment.

When Raymond and Tosh were in Italy, and their letters home finally reached Manzanar, it was Dorothy who read the letters to both of their families, and who shared stories of Tosh and Raymond's exploits with the Camp's guards as well as with other Japanese American families who were interned there.

So it was not surprising to anyone that Dorothy carried a torch for Raymond, i.e., she hoped – albeit secretly – that when he returned from Europe, he might ask her to marry him. As will be seen below, Raymond also harbored such thoughts.

17 - Robert's Wedding

In many ways Robert had been transformed by his studies under Father Roberge. The priest had been educated in Rome, and was steeped in the classics. That fact, especially when compared to the fundamentalist teachings Robert had received as a child from his parent's Methodist Church, appealed to him on an intellectual basis, and he was soon steeping himself in the writings of Catholic thinkers such as G. K. Chesterton (1874 - 1936) and John Henry Newman (1801 - 1890).

Indeed, and by the time Father Roberge was finished with Robert, Kathleen's brother Jim told his family that Robert had become more Catholic than the Catholics.

Robert seemed to confirm this in his Journal. He wrote, "As we approach the final term of our lives, it seems only fair to make clear our thanks to the Church and Almighty God for all of the many blessings we have received during the long and happy lives Kathleen and I have had together."

Robert's family was somewhat unhappy with his conversion to Catholicism. His parents had heard (and apparently believed) lurid tales spread about Catholics by itinerant "preachers" who claimed to be former priests and nuns. Indeed, Robert's father once asked his son (in a letter from Sacramento) if it were true that Catholic Priests insisted on the so-called right to a *nuit de seigneur* on the first night after a couple was married. An amused Robert assured his father that the answer to his question was a decisive no!

When the time came for their marriage ceremony, Robert had two men standing up for him, his friend, Doctor Al, and Kathleen's brother, Jim.

Kathleen's maids of honor were her two sisters, Noreen and Aileen, and her best friend, Marge Coleridge[33].

Two Irish Priests, Patrick O'Connell and Francis Walsh[34], presided over the ceremony, which was held at Saint Francis Church in suburban Melbourne.

Robert described his wedding in his Journal. "I remember standing at the altar as the music started I looked out over a sea of little girls in white veils (the Children

---

33. On April 2, 2012, Marge's son Mark was named Metropolitan Archbishop of Brisbane, Australia.

34. Both priests had been members of the IRA, and had left Ireland under a cloud during the Irish Civil War which followed Ireland's independence from the United Kingdom. As a young man, Father O'Connell was present at many speeches given by Padraig Pearce, including the speech which is presented in Chapter 1 of "The Early Troubles," (Seton Publishing, 1011). Later in life he stayed in touch with Kathleen, and spent many hours educating Kathleen's oldest son about the history of Ireland in the early 1900s.

of Mary), and the crowded church, and as I watched Kathleen make her way up the aisle, smiling and nodding to friends, I couldn't believe it was all happening to me. Fortunately, it was, and it did, and it was the greatest thing that could happen to me! Forty-five years, six wonderful children, and eighteen grandchildren later I still think so."

Festivities surrounding the wedding were uniformly happy and over the top, but there was a cloud hanging over the event. Everybody knew that Robert would soon be transferred north to join America's effort to take over the Japanese homeland.

Before the wedding, Kathleen's brother, Jim Salmon, asked Kathleen whether she really believed Robert would survive the war. Kathleen answered that she did, but in her heart, even she had her doubts.

18 - Camp Closure

In spite of the redactions of the Sunday editions of the *Los Angeles Times*, news stories of interest to the internees would occasionally slip by the Camp's censors. That was the case on June 3, 1945, when there was a news story about Manzanar. According to the story, the Camp would close at the end of November, 1945[35].

One month earlier, on May 8, 1945 (now known as "Victory in Europe" or "VE" Day), Allied forces had accepted Germany's unconditional surrender. That surrender, the apparent suicide of Adolph Hitler, and the execution of Benito Mussolini and his mistress by Italian partisans, meant that the War in Europe was now over.

Even though Japanese forces had suffered massive losses, the War in Asia was still raging, and many of the American troops fighting in Europe would soon be shipped east to join their fellow GI's in their assault on the Japanese homeland.

Mr. Ishi was puzzled when he read that Manzanar

---

35. In fact, the Camp formally closed on November 21, 1945.

would be closed before the War was over. "Why?" he thought to himself. "What have I missed?"

As a Camp representative, he decided to go to Major Butler, and ask him what was going on.

He knocked on the Major's door, and was admitted by the Major's wife. The Major recognized Mr. Ishi, and he asked him what was troubling him.

Mr. Ishi told him that he had read a report that the Camp was closing, and he wanted to know if it was true. The Major confirmed that it was, that he had just received word of the closure from the WRA, and that he would make a formal statement about the closure that evening after dinner.

Mr. Ishi asked him why the Camp was closing before the War was over, and the Major simply smiled. "It seems that the Supreme Court has now decided that innocent people cannot be held legally against their will." (See footnote 16 on page 16.)

That evening, Major Butler addressed the Camp's internee representatives. Here is what he had to say:

"Gentlemen. On behalf of the President of the United States, I have news of interest to you and your families. Pursuant to the laws of the United States, as interpreted by the Supreme Court, on or before November 30th of this year, the Manzanar Wartime Community will be officially and permanently closed. By reason of that closure, every person residing in this Community will be transported to Los Angeles at the Government's expense. From there you will be on your own, and free to travel to wherever you choose. You will not receive payment for your travels beyond Los Angeles, but you will have the thanks of the Government of the United States for your cooperation while you were housed at this Community."

At the end of the speech there was no applause or any other reaction. One by one the internee representatives simply turned around and walked back to their housing units.

19 - The Bomb

As the date of their August 4th wedding got closer, Robert and Kathleen were mindful of the danger that lay ahead.

American forces who had faced and fought the Japanese as the Allies moved closer to the Japanese homeland learned that forces loyal to the Emperor would fight to the death rather than surrender.

Of the 117,000 Japanese forces who defended Okinawa, ninety-four percent were killed or took their own lives rather than be captured by the Allies.

And experts who had analyzed the two phases of attack for Operation Downfall, which was the Allied plan for attacking the Japanese homeland[36], estimated that there would be somewhere between 1.7 and 4 million Allied casualties, of whom somewhere between 400,000 and 800,000 would lose their lives.

---

36. The first phase of the attack, on the southern island of Kyushu, was called Operation Olympic. The second phase of the attack, near Tokyo on the northern island of Honshu, was called Operation Coronet.

Robert had been notified by an advisory from his unit commander in early July 1945, that he and the rest of the American soldiers working at the Tooth's Brewery would be moved to Townsville in the north of Australia sometime in the next sixty days. There they would join an Allied battalion that would train them in hand-to-hand combat. And about a month after that, they would be shipped north to join other battalions for the Allied assault on Kyushu.

But then something truly amazing happened.

Two days after Robert and Kathleen were married, i.e., on August 6, 1945, the United States dropped an atomic bomb on the City of Hiroshima. And three days after that, it dropped a second atomic bomb on the City of Nagasaki[37]. Between the two bombs, it has been estimated that almost a quarter of a million people, most of whom were civilians, were killed.

People around the World were suddenly faced with the possibility that the War might end, and end immediately.

In Australia, the prospect of a possible end to the war with Japan was looked upon as Divine Intervention.

---

37. As a naval officer during the Vietnam War, the author visited "ground zero" for the bomb which destroyed Nagasaki. It was there that he learned that the point of greatest impact was a Catholic Church during a children's mass. Of the few remnants that survived the blast, the most notable were fragments of red stained glass that were melted into the small bones of young children who had otherwise been incinerated by the blast.

And while people in other countries debated (and still debate) the morality of dropping the two atomic bombs, Australians and members of the American military who were about to head north for the assault on the Japanese homeland were jubilant and unrepentant: to them, anything that ended the war was acceptable and appropriate.

In any case, at noon on August 15, 1945, the Japanese Emperor announced to his people and to the world at large that Japan had accepted a demand for surrender that had been delivered to his Cabinet by the Allies[38].

And a week after that, Robert was advised that his unit's advisory about proceeding north to Townsville had been rescinded, and that he and his fellow GI's should begin making plans to return home.

---

38. The formal surrender of Japan took place aboard the USS Missouri on September 2, 1945.

20 - *Raymond's Homecoming*

Raymond's homecoming was a matter of great excitement for his family. But it was also a matter of pride for the many thousands of Japanese Americans whose lives had been upended by their relocation of and incarceration.

Many had lost all of their possessions, and there was an undercurrent of resentment that more than a hundred thousand people had been punished solely on account of their ancestry.

On the other hand, the nation's press had followed the exploits of the 442nd with great interest, and on his first day back from Europe in late August of 1945, Raymond didn't know what to expect.

He had taken a train from New Jersey to California, and he had called ahead to see if his parents were back at their old home in Cupertino. To his relief, his family had returned home, and was already in the process of getting back to their old lives together.

He had also called ahead to see how Dorothy Sugiyama and her family were doing.

Tosh's death still weighed heavily on everyone. But there was good news as well. Dorothy, who had written to Raymond on a regular basis during all the time he was overseas, had assured Raymond that she was eager to see him. And she passed along the news that the Sugiyama family was flourishing once again.

During his first week back in San Jose, Raymond was asked by the City's Mayor to participate in a parade for returning veterans. Raymond agreed, and his family beamed with great pride when the Mayor, who had been a friend of Mr. Ishi before the war, announced from a stage that had been set up near City Hall that the people of California should take special notice of their favorite son, Major Raymond Ishimatsu, who had distinguished himself as a member of the 442nd, and was a recipient of not one but two Silver Stars!

The cheers from the crowd had become so loud that the parade was forced to stop, and the Mayor came down from the stage and gave Raymond a hug.

Later that day, Raymond was driven home in a family bus that had been used to carry workers on his family farm. It was covered with American Flags and a banner that proclaimed America's victory over its enemies.

A reception for more than one hundred persons, including Dorothy Sugiyama and her family, greeted Raymond with a standing ovation.

After the reception, Raymond went outside to inspect his family's orchards. And to his amazement, they looked as fresh and productive as ever. Raymond asked his father about this, but Mr. Ishi told his son they would discuss that later. (Please be patient: this will be clarified in Chapter 23).

Most important, of course, was Raymond's family. It turned out that they and most other internees had been released from Manzanar in late 1944, when the Supreme Court finally decided that innocents could not be incarcerated without charges against them.

In a gesture that was as insulting as it was inadequate, the American Government had eventually agreed to give each internee $25 to compensate them for expenses incurred in their travels back to their homes from Los Angeles.

The good news was that Raymond's parents and siblings all appeared to be happy and healthy, and not withstanding their tears, they had all pretty much returned to their pre-War lives.

21 - *Robert's Homecoming*

In the fall of 1945, shortly after Kathleen discovered she was pregnant, Robert was shipped back to the United States with the rest of his unit at Tooth's Brewery to be discharged in San Francisco.

As his troop ship steamed under the Golden Gate, Robert's heart was heavy. Speaking to his old friend, Doctor Al, Robert confided that he was overjoyed to be home at last, but he missed Kathleen, and was eager to see his new son, who had been born on Robert's thirtieth birthday.

As they were about to leave the ship, Robert asked his friend a favor. "I need to know something that you have never shared with me, even though I have asked it dozens of times. Who was it that authored the "All Hands" notice that resulted in my being transferred from New Guinea to the Tooth's Brewery in Melbourne?"

But as always, Doctor Al's response was to smile, and ask a question of his own: "How could I help it if you happened to fit the description of the kind of person I needed to get me through the War?"

Earlier that day, as their Troop Ship was taking on a pilot who would oversee the movement of the vessel toward San Francisco's Pier 35, Robert was handed a telegram by the ship's Yeoman. He opened the telegram, and discovered that it was from his family. Signed by his father, the telegram invited him and Doctor Al to a reception that would be held that evening at the Fairmont Hotel in downtown San Francisco.

And indeed, shortly after receiving his discharge papers, Robert left his troop ship with Doctor Al, and the two of them walked over to the Fairmont Hotel.

As they climbed Nob Hill on their way to the Fairmont, Robert asked Doctor Al what his plans were for the future.

"I supposed I could stay in the military," Al responded, "and if they keep promoting me, the next thing I know I'll be a general! The problem is that I've seen enough of the red tape it takes to get anything done in the Army, and for a change I'd like to practice medicine without somebody constantly looking over my shoulder. After all, that's why I went to medical school in the first place."

Robert nodded. "The truth is that I've already been contacted by a large canning company, and they have offered me a job as soon as my enlistment is over. It would be nice to make serious money for a change, and I'm going to accept their offer as soon as I can."

*   *   *   *   *

Theoretically, the Fairmont reception was meant to

honor Robert. But the real star was a handsome Major of Japanese American descent who was wearing an officer's dress uniform decorated with two Silver Stars. Of course, it was Robert's former roommate, Raymond, who was speaking with Robert's father and mother, and had just offered a toast to the memory of his friend, Tosh Sugiyama.

Upon seeing his parents, Robert gave each of them a hug. Then, with tears in his eyes, he turned to Raymond and the two men embraced each other. As they did so, the crowd began cheering wildly, and there was complete bedlam for several minutes.

Finally, as the cheering subsided, Robert asked Raymond if his parents were okay.

"Not only are they okay, but they are here to see you. And so is Carol."

And out from the back of the crowd stepped Mr. Ishi, Mom, and their daughter Carol. Robert grinned broadly, and there were long hugs with Raymond's family.

There were many more hugs, of course, and more visits with old friends, all of whose lives had been touched by the War, and many who had lost possessions – and family members – during the conflict.

Eventually things began to quiet down, and Raymond called over to Robert that he wanted to introduce him to someone.

"I want you to meet a lady who is very special to me." said Raymond. "Her name is Dorothy, and both of our families were friends at Manzanar. During my stay there, she and I fell in love, and it was she who was most responsible for my enlisting in the 442nd."

Robert couldn't help but notice that Dorothy was quite pretty, and that she was blushing.

Raymond continued, "We kept in touch during my service in Italy, and when I returned, I needed to make sure that some other guy wouldn't run off with her. So last week I proposed to her, and fortunately, she accepted. So, may I introduce you to my fiancé?"

Robert gave Dorothy a long hug, and once again he hugged Raymond.

"And I have one other order of business," said Raymond, pointing at Robert. "I was hoping you would be my best man."

"Nothing could make me happier," Robert responded. "I accept, and would be greatly honored."

And once again, everyone broke into a loud applause.

* * * * *

One month later, Raymond and Dorothy were married at the Buddhist Temple in San Jose. Robert was Raymond's best man, and Raymond's sister, Carol, was the Maid of Honor.

* * * * *

So it was that a relationship that had begun almost a decade earlier at UC Berkeley was restored, and Robert and Raymond would continue to be best friends for the next forty years.

Beginning in December 1947, and continuing every year until Robert retired in 1987, Raymond, Robert and their wives and children would get together between Christmas and New Year's Day, and the old friends would "conduct business" that consisted primarily of telling stories about life as it was experienced by them before, during, and after World War II.

22 - *Kathleen Sails to America*

Kathleen had always been close to her three siblings, and especially to her sister Aileen. As noted above, Aileen was an actress. But during the War she also worked as a private secretary for various politicians in the National Government. Pretty, intelligent and thoughtful, it was Aileen who helped Kathleen manage things in the months that followed her marriage[39].

Robert had left Australia in October of 1945, when his Unit was shipped back to California. Kathleen was eager to join him, of course, but she was pregnant, and she wanted to wait until her baby was born before she took one of the many troop ships that were taking so-called "war brides" to the United States to join their

---

39. Aileen, who passed away when she was well into her nine-ties, had married an Australian, Daniel Moriarty, shortly after the War. Daniel died young, but not before their beautiful daughter, Kathleen, came into their lives. Kathleen and her husband, Alan, produced many children of their own, some of whom have made their way to the United States, where they are a constant source of entertainment and good humor.

American husbands[40].

In June of 1946, Kathleen's baby, a boy, was born (on Robert's 30th birthday) in Bethlehem Hospital in Caulfield, and Kathleen immediately applied for transport to the United States. Shortly thereafter she was notified that she would be boarding the S. S. Marine Falcon in Melbourne Harbor on October 1, 1946, and she and her son would be taking a three week voyage that would terminate in San Francisco.

In the weeks before she left for America, Kathleen's house in Elsternwick was continually filled with friends she had made over the years. Many of these, of course, were members of the Therry Society, including novelist Morris West.

The night before she left for America, she attended a huge reception arranged by her sister, Aileen, at the theater where most of the Therry Society productions were staged.

Tears were everywhere, especially at the end when Aileen introduced Kathleen's three-month old son to the crowd, and they ended the evening by singing "Waltzing Matilda," an Australian "bush ballad" written by poet Banjo Paterson in 1895, which had been

---

40. These troop ships included war brides from New Zealand and Australia, but they also carried many Japanese nationals who had married Allied soldiers in the immediate aftermath of the Japanese surrender.

popular at the end of the War as friends became separated, perhaps forever[41]. In the song, a drifter with all his possessions in a "matilda" or duffel-like backpack is walking through the outback, looking for work, and waiting for his "billie" or cooking pot, to boil. In Paterson's words:

> *Waltzing Matilda, Waltzing Matilda, You'll come a-Waltzing Matilda, with me. And he sang as he watched, and waited 'til his billie boiled. You'll come a-Waltzing Matilda, with me.*

On the day of her departure, Kathleen waved goodbye to a crowd of about one hundred friends, including her parents and siblings, and boarded the troop ship that would take her first to Tahiti, then Hawaii, and finally to San Francisco.

Many of the war brides on board the Marine Falcon had young children with them, and one of the brides, a pretty brunette from New Zealand named Gloria Walton, developed a close friendship with Kathleen in the course of the voyage. Indeed, for decades thereafter, Aunt Gloria and Uncle Bill Walton and their children were regular fixtures at any Rose family gathering.

The three week trip to America was arduous, of course, but by the time they arrived in San Francisco, Kathleen

---

41. When Kathleen died many years later, one of her many granddaughters, Katie, sang "Waltzing Matilda" at her funeral in Sacramento's Holy Spirit Church. On this occasion, too, there wasn't a dry eye in the house.

had forgotten about the sea sickness that had plagued her for much of the early part of her voyage, and the sleepless nights she had to endure with her young son. Her friend Gloria had been a tireless companion to Kathleen, and by the time their trip had ended, both women wanted nothing more than to go to bed and get some well-deserved sleep while somebody else took care of their babies.

On the day their ship tied up along the San Francisco Marina, Kathleen was met by Robert, of course, but also by his family. They included a brother, Norman, a sister, Winifred, and both of Robert's parents, Edgar and Pearl Rose. But Raymond and his wife, Dorothy, were also there, as were I. K. and Mom Ishimatsu. Kathleen was well aware of the hardships that had been endured by the Ishimatsu family during the War, and she was surprised to find them as happy as they were.

Xenophobia was not unheard of during the War, even in Australia, but Kathleen made it clear that she welcomed the Ishimatus as though they were members of her family. And indeed, they remained so for the rest of their lives.

*   *   *   *   *

Life in America must have been something of a challenge for Kathleen.

After years of almost frenetic activity, she was suddenly stuck at home with no automobile (much less a driver), no maid, no nanny, and few friends.

Nobody she knew played tennis or golf, and she wouldn't have had the time to engage in sports, even if there were opportunities to do so.

With her husband at work, and often out of town, she had no resources for dealing with broken appliances and other routine challenges that she faced around her home.

The informality of life in California was particularly disconcerting for her, and she was shocked that people wouldn't dress up before they went shopping in Sacramento's central shopping area. In fact, it was years before she finally gave up trying to force Robert to wear a sports coat at their nightly dinners together[42].

Although she had never seen black Aborigines when she was living in Australia[43], she was shocked by the rudeness which white people in California showed to American blacks.

She was amazed when Americans would express their surprise that someone from Australia could speak English as well as she did.

She was dismayed at the lack of knowledge or even of interest shown by most Californians when it came to live theater productions, the arts, and classic literature.

---

42. By the sixties, informality at evening meals had eventually degenerated to the point that all of her six children wore nothing more than skimpy Speedo racing swimsuits.

43. In the 1930s and 1940s, Aborigines seldom left the safety and climate of Northern Australia. And even if they did, they seldom made it as far south as the State of Victoria.

As a young actress in Australia, Kathleen was known as "Thursday Night Kal" because she could read a script on Thursday, and perform it two days later on Saturday[44]. Decades later, in her life as a mother and wife, she still had almost perfect recall, but nobody else around her seemed to have that gift, and it was frustrating for Robert and their children to deal with someone who always knew what you (and she) had said about any subject.

Kathleen was particularly appalled by the prejudice shown against any racial or religious group, and she would go ballistic if she learned that someone she knew had joined a club that was "restricted" in its membership[45].

As did most Catholics at the time, Kathleen lionized Jack and Jackie Kennedy, and when the President was assassinated in November of 1963, she created a miniature shrine to the fallen President which consisted of a

---

44. This remarkable gift was also possessed by her mother, Florence Anne Jolley, her daughter, Anne Gabrielle Rose, and her granddaughter, Anne Elizabeth Rose. Why that gift devolved to four generations of women, and not to any of the males in the family, is a mystery. Perhaps it had something to do with the name "Anne."

45. A "restricted" club was one which barred membership to a class of individuals, including Jews, Blacks and Asians. Needless to say, nobody in her family, much less Robert, ever dared to express a desire to join a country club, since virtually all country clubs in the Sacramento area barred entry to somebody.

photograph of the President and a votive candle. She placed it on a small table (next to a treasured statue of the Blessed Mother that she had brought with her from Australia[46]) in the entry room to her home.

As a Democrat, Kathleen was frustrated when, after acquiring American citizenship in 1954, Robert's family (which consisted solely of Republicans) espoused political positions that ran counter to basic tenets that were accepted by virtually all Australians, i.e., national health care, universal suffrage, and gender equality in political and professional life.

Fiercely religious, Kathleen made her children go to mass every day during Lent, Advent, and Holy Week[47]. She also made them kneel on the floor every evening after dinner, and recite the Rosary. And once a month, on the First Friday, everyone had to go to Confession, and then to Church for Benediction.

Needless to say, all these masses and other Catholic

---

46. At some point the late 1960s the statue was knocked off the table by one of Kathleen's children, and the head was separated from the rest of the statue's body. Undeterred, Kathleen had the head mounted separately on a new base, and it continued in its place of honor.

47. For readers who didn't grow up Catholic, "Lent" is the six week period between Ash Wednesday and Holy Thursday, three days before Easter. "Advent" is the period between the fourth Sunday before Christmas ("Advent Sunday") and Christmas day.

rituals were quite time consuming, and over the years they created a certain amount of resentment on the part of Kathleen's children.

But by the time she developed Alzheimer's Disease in the 1990s, Kathleen had stopped enforcing many of the religious practices she had insisted on when her family was young, and for the most part, her children had shed the negative feelings that they had harbored about the Catholic Church.

Near the end of her life, as her mind began to fail, Kathleen accepted the idea that her American family was less religious, less formal, less cultured, and less well read than she was.

She also learned to accept (if not embrace) the Beatles, Bob Dylan, and several other rock-'n-roll artists that she would play on a large record player that she and Robert had purchased for their living room. Indeed, on several occasions she even accompanied one or more of her children to rock concerts.

But she could never quite accept Jimmy Hendrix, especially when he played "The Star-Spangled Banner" on his electric guitar using his teeth to pick out the basic notes of the song.

Nonetheless, and except for her Australian accent which persisted to the end, and her love of classical music, she eventually became as American as anyone. And she liked it that way.

23 - The Bank

As promised in Chapter 5, this will conclude the story of what happened to the assets of thousands of Japanese Americans that were accepted by A. P. Giannini and his Bank through the issuance of trust agreements which were agreed to by families that were about to be shipped to internment camps.

The author learned about the outcome from his father, Robert Rose, who was reunited with his old friend, Raymond Ishimatsu, at the end of the war. Both men had gone into the produce business, and although they worked for different entities, they continued to maintain close contact with one another for the rest of their lives.

According to Raymond, when the War ended, Mr. Ishi and the others who had entrusted their assets to the Bank were called together for another meeting held at the San Jose Civic Auditorium.

The same man who had spoken to the soon-to-be internees in early 1942, A. P. Giannini, was still involved in the management of the Bank, whose name had been changed over time to the Bank of America[48].

This time his sound system was working, and he had a grim look on his face. "My friends," he started off. "I know that many of you have suffered greatly at the hands of our Government, and there are no words I could use to say what I feel in my heart. But please give me a few minutes to express the sorrow I feel over the injustice that has been done to you and your families. When we last spoke in early 1942, I cited the Constitution of the United States, and expressed regret at the violations of the rights promised you by that Constitution. Sadly, there is nothing I can do to make up for the injustice wreaked upon you by those violations. But I can do something else that you are entitled to under the "Trust Agreements" you signed – many under great pressure – half a decade ago. I can keep my word, and that is exactly what I am going to do right now."

With that, he pointed to a series of tables that had been set up on the stage next to him.

"On each of those tables is a portfolio, all of which have been stacked alphabetically for your convenience, and each portfolio is embossed in gold leaf with the name of every family that signed a Trust Agreement on the day we last met. Inside each of the portfolios is a comprehensive accounting of each and every possession that you entrusted to the Bank's care in 1942, a statement of the value of those possessions when entrusted to us,

---

48. A. P. Giannini died on June 3, 1949, in San Mateo, California.

and a statement of present value. The bulk of each port-folio is made up of records that document each pur-chase and sale that was completed in your name, and an explanation by the Bank in its fiduciary capacity for all income attributed to your account."

Once again, as in 1942, when Mr. Giannini finished his remarks, he was met with prolonged silence. But one by one, the family representatives who were present that day began to walk up to the stage.

Over the next hour or so, as the former internees read the summary pages of their portfolios, tears of joy appeared on their faces. It had become obvious that to the person, <u>every</u> <u>one</u> who had entrusted their assets to the Bank, had significantly increased their wealth, and some had done so well beyond their wildest dreams.

Some were so overcome with joy that they embraced Mr. Giannini and wouldn't let him go.

Mr. Ishi, among others, discovered that his orchards had not only flourished, but had been expanded. And to his surprise, the Bank had invested in a Japanese res-taurant that was now wholly owned by the Ishimatsu family, and was generating more money than the fam-ily's orchards.

Finally, a former internee whose son had served with Raymond in the 442nd, walked up to the lectern, and asked for those present to applaud Giannini.

The crowd responded immediately, generating, accord-ing to one report, the longest and most enthusiastic round of applause any of them had ever heard.

* * * * *

Years later the author was at a business meeting with a senior officer of the Bank of America. He was quite elderly, but alert, and obviously bright, with clear recollections.

He told the author that he had worked directly for Mr. Giannini. So the author asked him if the stories he had heard about the internees, their trust agreements, and the meetings at the San Jose Civic Auditorium, before and after the interments, were true.

The officer asked to hear the stories that the author had heard, and was given the descriptions that are retold in this book. After hearing the stories he confirmed that they actually happened as had been told to the author. But he went further.

He added that the families of many of those same internees, including later generations, still do their banking with the Bank of America, and would never do business with any other Bank – including Japanese banks – because Mr. Giannini had kept his word.

<u>24 - Afterward</u>

After the War, Mr. Ishi and Mom, who both lived into their nineties, turned their attention to the restaurant that had been purchased in their family's name by the Bank of America. It still exists near a street in San Jose, since renamed "Ishimatsu Place."

Robert's father died in 1952, but his mother lived into her nineties, and died in Sacramento in 1982. His paternal grandmother died shortly before the War ended in 1945, and his maternal grandparents lived into their nineties, and died just a few months from each other in 1957.

After his discharge from the Army, Raymond took over his father's farming operation, and he ran it until he retired in the mid 1980s. In the decade that followed the end of the War, Raymond and Dorothy produced five daughters, all of whom were raised in Santa Clara County. Raymond died in San Jose in 2011 at the age of 87.

His wife, Dorothy, and his sister, Carol, are both still living at the time this book is being published.

As for Robert, he and his Australian bride eventually produced six children, all of whom were raised in Sacramento, California. Kathleen died of complications from Alzheimer's disease in Woodland, California in October, 2003. She was 84.

Robert died – apparently of a broken heart – three months later, in Yuba City, California, at the age of 87.

After his discharge, Doctor Al moved to the east coast, and as he wanted, he opened a family medical practice on Cape Cod in the City of Chatham. He eventually married a local lady who taught history at a community college near Boston, and they lived happily together, without any children, until they both died in their mid-seventies.

25 - One Last Matter

Those of you who are animal lovers might wonder what eventually happened to Robert's pet pig, Betty.

On the day Robert and Kathleen were married, Betty was left for several hours in the backyard of the home of Kathleen's parents. Unfortunately, Betty took advantage of being left alone, and she managed to eat most of the flowers in the Salmon family's garden[49].

Later, and despite Betty's misbehavior during Robert and Kathleen's wedding, all was forgiven.

In early 1946, when Robert and Doctor Al were about to be returned with their Unit to the United States,[50] on a so-called "Victory Ship," Doctor Al used the same device Robert had used he when left New Guinea on his

---

49. The Salmon home was located at 80 St. George's Road in Elsternwick, a suburb of Melbourne in the Australian State of Victoria.

50. In this case, the troop ship which carried them home was the USS Pachaug Victory, which was jammed with almost 15,000 GI's.

way to Australia.

According to a reliable source who overheard the discussion, he supposedly gifted the Captain with a bottle of fifty-year-old Irish Whiskey. He then convinced him that Betty was a "bonza research animal"[51], and it was on that basis (not to mention the fact that she was his Unit's official mascot) that Betty should be allowed to travel to America with Robert and Doctor Al.

Ultimately, the Captain agreed. And as a consequence, Betty was permitted to tag along for the voyage, but only on the condition that Doctor Al promised to keep her in his cabin – which he did.

When they reached the United States, and Robert and Doctor Al were both discharged, Robert took Betty to Sacramento, where she lived for a brief time with his

---

51. In case the reader isn't conversant with Australian slang, something "bonza" is exceptionally good. Other examples of Australian slang include the words "plonk" (cheap wine), a "dog's breakfast" (messy), "fay" (fairy like), a "bogan" (a redneck), "do the Harry" (disappear, as did Prime Minister Harold Holt, who was – perhaps – eaten by a white shark while swimming off the coast of Victoria; see footnote 25 of "Hamilton & Egberta," Seton Publishing, 2017), "chockers" (very full), "fair dinkum" (genuine), "ripper" (really good), "Aussie" (an Australian), "Oz" (Australia), and "Kiwi"(someone from New Zealand). And then there is the slang word "root." Because this is a family book, I won't translate this word, so don't ask what it means. I will only say that its Australian meaning is quite vulgar, and that most Aussies laugh like crazy when they hear American baseball fans sing in unison that they want to "root, root, root for the home team".

parents on 42nd Street.

Later, when Robert purchased his first home on Sacramento's V Street, Betty was re-settled in a chicken coop that Robert built in his back yard. As far as Robert could tell, the chicken coop was sound, and there was no danger that Betty would escape and attack any of his neighbors, even if she were somehow inclined in that direction (which she wasn't).

While on V Street,[52] Betty lived a long and happy life as the Rose family's pet, while city officials (who were supposed to keep wild animals out of residential areas) looked the other way. After all, Betty wasn't really "wild," and was probably domesticated, and, in any case, she was an Army celebrity after she appeared in *Stars and Stripes* as the Unit Mascot of Camp Theodore Roosevelt in New Guinea.

In any case, a Sacramento city official eventually contacted Robert "off the record," and told him that Betty was safe and that her status would not be challenged by the City. According to the official, an informal survey by the City had determined that Betty was more popular than the Mayor. Apparently that survey was more significant to the City Council than its ban on "wild "animals.

Over the next few years, it was not unusual for perfect strangers to stop by Robert and Kathleen's home, and

---

52. V Street, which was located near Sacramento High School, was torn up and replaced in the 1970s by what is now a freeway.

ask to take pictures of Betty. In fact, Betty's photograph was displayed on the pages of both of Sacramento's daily newspapers, the *Sacramento Bee* and the *Sacramento Union*.

On one occasion, an entire Kindergarten class from nearby Newton Booth School, stopped by to see Betty, and to feed her candy treats.

But Betty was mostly unfazed by her notoriety, and when she was let out of the chicken coop from time to time, she seemed content to follow Robert and Kathleen's children in walks around the block.

Not surprisingly, and for the rest of her life, Betty's favorite activity in her role as the Rose family pet was eating desert each evening which consisted of powdered ice cream.

<u>*Credits*</u>

As with my previous books, I thank my family for their patience and support for the time I take from all of our lives to pursue my love of writing.

I would also like to thank my brother Jim, who is well acquainted with most of the stories that have found their way into my narrative.

Finally, and as always, I would like to thank Tony Seton whose dogged support and constant optimism are an important part of my creative process.

The Author

A native of Australia, Gerard Rose is a trial lawyer, sometime politician, and an advocate for a wide variety of noble and important civic causes. His higher education included stints at the University of Santa Clara, and the Rome campus of Loyola University.

As an officer in the United States Navy during the 1960s, Gerard traveled throughout the western Pacific, including Vietnam. In the early 1970s he taught international law and national strategy to senior naval officers.

Over the years he has served as a scout leader, PTA president, a director of his children's grammar school, a council member and vice mayor of his local City Council, a director of his city's Redevelopment Agency, president of his city's fire/ambulance authority, president of his city's Art Gallery Alliance, a director of his city's cultural arts center, and as Deputy City Attorney of the City of Carmel-by-the-Sea.

He is married to a clinical psychologist, and he has five children and four grandchildren. He commutes regularly between California and Illinois, and while in the air he can usually be found reading trashy novels.

SETON
PUBLISHING

92000151R00071

Made in the USA
San Bernardino, CA
28 October 2018